Hachette UK's policy is to use papers that are natural, renewable and recyclable products and made from wood grown in well-managed forests and other controlled sources. The logging and manufacturing processes are expected to conform to the environmental regulations of the country of origin.

ISBN: 9781398324329

Text © Adam and Charlotte Guillain
Illustrations, design and layout © Hodder and Stoughton Ltd
First published in 2022 by Hodder & Stoughton Limited (for its Rising Stars imprint, part of the Hodder Education Group),
An Hachette UK Company
Carmelite House 50 Victoria Embankment London EC4Y 0DZ
www.risingstars-uk.com

Impression number 10 9 8 7 6 5 4 3 2 1
Year 2026 2025 2024 2023 2022

Author: Adam and Charlotte Guillain
Series Editor: Tony Bradman
Commissioning Editor: Hamish Baxter
Illustrator: Katie Kear/Bright International Group
Educational Reviewer: Helen Marron
Design concept: David Bates
Page layouts: Rocket Design (East Anglia) Ltd
Editor: Amy Tyrer

With thanks to the schools that took part in the development of *Reading Planet* KS2, including: Ancaster CE Primary School, Ancaster; Downsway Primary School, Reading; Ferry Lane Primary School, London; Foxborough Primary School, Slough; Griffin Park Primary School, Blackburn; St Barnabas CE First & Middle School, Pershore; Tranmoor Primary School, Doncaster; and Wilton CE Primary School, Wilton.

A catalogue record for this title is available from the British Library.

Printed in the United Kingdom

Orders: Please contact Hachette UK Distribution, Hely Hutchinson Centre, Milton Road, Didcot, Oxfordshire, OX11 7HH.

Telephone: (44) 01235 400555. Email: primary@hachette.co.uk.

Contents

1 Next Stop, the Wild Unknown . . 4

2 The Death Slide 21

3 Orienteering 32

4 Into the Woods 40

5 The Long Trek Home 55

1 Next Stop, the Wild Unknown

The day of the Year 6 trip had finally arrived. It wasn't even 7 o'clock in the morning when Sara's dad dropped her off with her bags.

"You're not going to believe it!" Sara told Lexi, as they took their seats on the coach. "I can't go to Rosedale."

"You're kidding, right?" said Lexi.

Everybody Sara knew was planning to go to Rosedale Secondary School next year.

"But your new flat isn't even that far away," said Lexi.

"It makes no difference," said Sara. "Mum read me the letter this morning. I'm going to Nelson Mandela High."

"Well, that's totally ruined my day," Lexi grumbled. "Great."

"It's not my fault," said Sara. "I didn't choose to go to another school!"

"I didn't say you did!" Lexi snapped. "It's just rubbish news."

Carter arrived in a car with Ethan. Sara felt tense thinking what he would say when he heard her news.

"This trip is going to be the best!" said Carter, throwing himself down onto a seat across the aisle.

"Sara's going to Nelson Mandela High School in September," said Lexi, in a posh voice.

"No!" gasped Carter, his mouth open. "Why?"

"It's not my idea!" Sara snapped. "Our new flat isn't in the right catchment area for Rosedale."

"Well, that's it then," said Carter. "You're breaking up the group. We'll never see you now."

Sara felt hurt that neither of them was thinking about how she felt. She'd been hoping to make the best of things this week. If it was going to be the last trip they were ever going to have together, it had to be a good one.

For once, Carter was quiet for a bit. Sara examined his face, trying to work out how he was feeling. The way he just blurted things out was such a pain sometimes. Usually, because he was right.

"Femi's here," said Carter, watching Femi get out of a taxi and heave out his bag. "He's not going to like Sara's news. He was really looking forward to this trip. He really needs it!"

Femi had been having a tough time all year, caring for his mum.

Sara wanted to scream. All of them were looking forward to this trip – not just Femi. The news that she wasn't going to Rosedale shouldn't have to ruin everything.

"OMG!" Carter guffawed, pointing to a small blue car. An even more brightly-coloured figure was stepping out of it. "Mrs Wilde's wearing jeans! And she's got a hoodie on too!"

"LOL! She looks so much younger!" Lexi spluttered.

Children and teachers were arriving quickly now. Sara was relieved. At least the conversation seemed to be veering away from her news.

"Sara's going to that posh school," Carter told Femi as he sat down.

"Not Nelson Mandela High?" gasped Femi with a disbelieving grin. "Nah – she wouldn't do that. Sara's going to Rosedale. She's one of us, isn't she?" He looked across at Sara.

"Not for much longer," said Carter, holding up his arms in a shrug.

"Oh," sighed Femi, his grin disappearing. "It's your new flat, isn't it? I knew it would ruin everything."

Sara's eyes started to well up, so she turned away and stared out of the window. Her friends meant the world to her. Why didn't they understand how upset she felt? This trip wasn't going the way she wanted and they hadn't even left school yet!

"I'm still not sure about Rosedale," Sara heard Femi whisper to Carter. "Do you think it will be all right?"

"Not if you're going to go around worrying about it all the time," said Carter. "So what if the big kids think they can boss us around? We'll show them that they can't!"

Sara knew Femi was nervous about Rosedale, but at least he was going to have some friends there. She didn't know anyone else going to Nelson Mandela High.

"Hey – look!" Carter laughed, gesturing to Mr Kaminski and Mrs Coats as they stepped on to the bus wearing matching tracksuits.

Sara sank back in her seat and wished she was somewhere else.

When Mr Ali got on to the bus carrying his guitar and wearing jeans and a cartoon T-shirt, there was a buzz of excitement. Carter leaned over the seat in front and started to rap loudly.

Within seconds, Lexi was out of her seat and clapping along.

"We're going on a trip,
our teachers look hip.
Our teachers are in hoodies
or in tracksuits with a zip!"

Sara thought Mr Ali looked stressed as he headed down the aisle towards them.

"Lexi, sit down!" she whispered, pulling at Lexi's arm.

"We're going on a trip and we're staying up all night. No one's going to tell us what to do – all right?" Carter finished.

"Stop!" said Mr Ali. "No, Carter, it's not all right."

Carter stopped. "I'd already finished, anyway," he said.

"Carter and Lexi, save the singing for the campfire please," said Mr Ali. "If you're going to continue mucking about this morning, let me remind you there are classrooms at the activity centre. I have lots of worksheets with me."

Sara gave Lexi a worried look when she sat down.

"I don't think stressing Mr Ali out is a good idea," she told Lexi.

When Lexi didn't answer, Sara started to worry she had annoyed her friend.

"It's weird when you see teachers out of school," she said to her friend, trying to think of something they could laugh about together. "They always look so different."

"I know, right," said Lexi, grinning. "I once saw Mr Ali playing in a football match at the park. He was shouting stuff like 'Over here!' and 'Come on lads!' and it just felt wrong."

When the driver put the radio on and started to drive, the children began waving to all the sleepy-eyed parents who had hung around to see them off.

"Next stop, the wild unknown," Mrs Wilde cheered.

Slowly, the general buzz of loud excitement gave way to yawns and chatter.

As the bus headed out of the city, Sara started to think about the days ahead.

At least Mr Ali had kept them all in their friendship groups for the trip. Perhaps if all the activities went well, they'd have a really good time. Friends who had good times together didn't fall out – whichever secondary school they were going to.

"What are you thinking about?" asked Lexi.

Sara wondered how long Lexi had been looking at her.

"All the stuff we might be doing at the activity centre," said Sara.

"Me too!" cried Lexi, her eyes ablaze. "The zipwire there has an extra-long drop, which makes it super fast! They call it the death slide!"

"Really?" said Sara, feeling sick. "How high is it?"

"*Really* high!" said Carter, his eyes wide. "I heard that some kids are so scared when they see it, they get dizzy and sick."

"Where did you hear that?" Sara asked in a panic.

"From this boy I know who goes to Rosedale," said Carter. "He says there are wild scary animals in the forest, too."

"Like what?" said Sara, wondering how wild and scary they could be.

"Use your imagination," said Carter.

"Big creepy-crawlies," said Lexi with a grimace. "And snakes!"

"Look," said Carter crossly. "If the zipwire and forest aren't a bit scary, what's the point? We may as well sit on the swings and watch squirrels in the park."

Sara didn't agree. The activities she had been looking forward to were the night walks and the birdwatching. Now she was thinking of all the scary wild animals Carter couldn't wait to see.

It was lunchtime when the coach turned on to the long driveway that led to Ripley Fields Outward Bound Centre.

The children found their bags and placed them on their bunks in the dormitories. Then they had a packed lunch on the grass outside.

"Right," said Mr Ali when they'd finished eating. "Time for me to introduce you to Meg, who is team leader here at Ripley Fields."

Meg welcomed everyone to the centre and went through a few safety rules. Then she introduced them to her team: Gary, Alison, Ivan and River.

"Right," said Mr Ali, calming everyone down. "Time to give each team a name, a leader and their first task."

"He's bound to pick you as our leader," Sara told Lexi. "You're already captain of all those sports teams."

"Do you think?" said Lexi with a hopeful smile.

"And remember," Mr Ali said, "each team will be assessed on performance and teamwork for every activity. At the end of the trip, there'll be a prize for the winning team."

"We're going to win this!" someone called out.

Sara saw that the voice had come from Ethan, who was now busy talking to his friend Sol. She felt a nudge.

"If those boys think their group is going to beat us, they're going to get a shock," Lexi muttered.

She had a very determined look on her face.

"They've got Ryan in their group too, so they've got a good chance," said Carter.

Reading from his clipboard, Mr Ali called out the names of the six children he had chosen to lead their teams. Sure enough, Ethan was the first team leader to be named.

Sara listened and watched as one by one, each team was given a leader and the name of a tree.

"Who do you think our team leader will be?" asked Femi, as Dina-May walked to the front to pick up her instructions as the leader of Beech team.

"Lexi," said Carter.

"Carter," said Lexi.

"And finally, our group of four," said Mr Ali, looking up from his clipboard with a twinkle in his eyes. "The leader of the Alder team is Sara."

"What?" gasped Sara with a flinch. "Me?"

"Sara?" exclaimed Carter loudly.

Sara felt her whole body tensing up.

"But why not Lexi?" Carter called out as Sara stumbled up to collect the team's instructions.

When Sara finally got to the front, Mr Ali handed her an envelope.

"This is going to be a great challenge for you, Sara," Mr Ali said with a smile.

Sara wanted to tell him that she really didn't need another challenge at the moment. Moving flat and dealing with going to Nelson Mandela High next year were more than enough.

When Sara opened the envelope, she found a site map and a set of instructions. She gasped.

"Sorry," she said, shooting off to the dormitory with the instructions in her hand. "I didn't know I'd need my reading glasses. I'll be quick!"

"Just hurry up!" Carter called after her.

By the time Sara got back, Carter and Lexi looked restless.

"All the other groups have read their instructions already," Carter complained.

"Don't listen to Carter," said Femi. "He thinks everything's a race."

"Well, it is!" shouted Lexi. "We want to win this thing, right?"

Sara had never seen Lexi look so irritated.

"I don't even want to be team leader," Sara protested. "Lexi, why don't you do it?"

"No – just get on with it," said Femi. "If Mr Ali sees us arguing, we'll never win this thing."

"He's right," said Lexi. "Come on, Sara. Read!"

Sara fumbled her glasses on and got out the map. She quickly scanned the instructions.

"We need to be wearing trainers and be at the foot of Rockford Falls at 2:15," she told them.

"But I've got my wellies on," moaned Carter.

"Me too," said Femi.

"Typical!" groaned Lexi, who already had her trainers on. "Go and get them quickly while I look at the map and work out how to get there."

"Why are *you* suddenly in charge?" said Femi. "That's Sara's job."

19

"Sara doesn't even want to be leader," Carter moaned, wandering off.

"Hurry up!" exclaimed Lexi.

Sara hoped Lexi wouldn't notice the tears in her eyes as she watched her friend reading the map.

"Rockford Falls – got it!" Lexi exclaimed. "We're going on the death slide!"

Sara felt sick with dread.

\#2 The Death Slide

By the time Femi and Carter got back, Lexi was already marching off ahead of them all, waving the map.

"I suppose we better catch up with her," Femi panted.

"No way!" said Carter, walking slowly. "Lexi can't go around acting like she's the boss."

Sara was too upset to argue and hurried to catch up with Lexi.

With Lexi firmly holding on to the map, she led them all down a long track through the trees. Eventually they arrived at a large lake, where Ethan and his team were gathered around kayaks listening to Gary from the activity centre.

"Look!" Femi gasped, pointing at a long zipwire that ran from a point above the lake right down to the shallows by the boathouse.

"The death slide!" Lexi cheered, her face beaming.

"It's not really called that," said Femi, shaking his head. "That's just crazy kid talk."

Sara gaped up at the summit. Crazy kid talk or not, she didn't want to do it.

Lexi checked the map and started to run uphill.

"Follow me!" she shouted.

Alison, another instructor, was waiting for them all at the base of Rockford Falls.

"Well done," she said cheerily when Sara and the others finally caught up with Lexi. "This first activity is a team obstacle course, ending with a zipwire down to the lakeside."

Sara stared at the climbing walls and ropes and all the other weird-looking obstacles around the course. She gulped.

"Is it a race?" asked Lexi eagerly.

"It's a team race, like all the activities," said Alison. "Your team leader needs to make sure you work together to complete the course."

"What does that mean?" asked Lexi grumpily.

"It means that your team's time starts now. It stops when the last member takes the zipwire down to the boathouse," Alison explained, getting out her stopwatch. "I'll meet you at the end of the obstacle course. Now, go!"

Sara faltered as Carter and Lexi dived into the tunnels that led to the first climbing wall.

"Why are they being so competitive?" Sara grumbled. "I thought we were supposed to be having fun!"

"Shall we stick together?" Femi asked. "I've never done this before."

"Me neither," said Sara. "Let's help each other."

"I hate this kind of thing," Femi panted as he emerged from the first tunnel.

"I know," said Sara, pulling him. "Don't worry, you're doing great."

Sara and Femi both found the rope ladders on the first wall difficult to climb. Looking down from the top of the wall, Sara felt dizzy and scared. But she still managed to reach down and help Femi up.

Once they'd crossed all the walls and obstacles, Sara and Femi ran up the rest of the hill to the zipwire.

"Are you all right, Sara?" Femi panted when they got to the top. "You look a bit sick."

24

"It's too high up," groaned Sara.

"Well done," Alison told them as they caught their breath. "I've been watching you two help each other. This part of the team is working really well together."

Mrs Wilde was waiting, wearing a pink jacket and holding a harness. "Right, we need to get you two down this zipwire quickly and safely. Lexi and Carter couldn't wait to get down."

Sara watched Femi put his helmet and harness on. She'd felt like she had a friend when they were on the obstacle course together. But now Femi had forgotten about how nervous she was. He flew off down the wire, screaming excitedly. Sara was on her own.

She felt annoyed with herself for being so scared. Then, Mrs Wilde beckoned her to come forwards.

Sara panicked. "I can't do it," she quivered, backing away. "It's too high up here. I feel dizzy."

Mrs Wilde smiled kindly. "You know, Sara, Mr Ali and I think you've done really well this year."

Sara had no idea what Mrs Wilde was talking about. It was obvious to Sara that all her friends had done amazing things. Lexi was great at sports, Carter was brilliant at music and Femi was a maths genius. But what had she done that was any good? Nothing!

"I saw the way you led Femi through the obstacle course," said Mrs Wilde. "And what makes it more remarkable is that you did it while being scared of heights."

Sara knew Mrs Wilde was trying to say something nice. But she couldn't help thinking it was just the headteacher's way of encouraging her to get on with it.

"But I can't do *that!*" Sara trembled, pointing at the zipwire.

"I know this is hard," said Mrs Wilde. "The others didn't need to be brave to do this, but you do. If you do it, I just know you'll be relieved and feel really proud of yourself."

Sara let Mrs Wilde clip her into the harness.

"When you're ready, you can go," said Mrs Wilde.

Sara was clutching her harness so tightly it was hurting her hands. She closed her eyes and breathed deeply several times. "I can do this," she told herself.

And then she pushed herself away.

The cool rush of air hitting her face felt electric. She opened her eyes and felt a rush of excitement. *This is amazing!* she thought as she flew down towards the lake. Before she knew it, she was splashing through the shallows with an urge to do the whole thing again. The wonderful feeling vanished when she saw the look on her friends' faces.

"What took you so long?" cried Lexi.

"Let's try and catch up on the next activity," said Carter with a shrug.

Sara felt her happy bubble pop. It was going to be impossible to enjoy this trip if she kept slowing everyone down. By the time it was over, her friends would probably be glad she wasn't going to Rosedale with them.

As the groups finished their afternoon activities, they started making their way back to the activity centre.

Sara thought Lexi might walk back with her, but she ran off ahead with Carter.

When she got back to the centre, Sara saw Meena and Brianna carrying wood to the firepit and went to join them.

"What have you been doing?" Sara asked them.

"We went mountain biking with River," said Brianna, throwing down her wood. "We cycled for miles and went past this marsh and saw herons and all kinds of stuff."

"I saw a black-tailed godwit!" said Meena. "River told me I was the keenest bird-spotter he'd seen here all year!"

"I heard that the Ash team did orienteering and they all got soaked in the river," said Brianna.

Just then, Sol came bounding over.

"You're all going to L.O.V.E. love the kayaking," he told them. "That man called Gary is actually called Gazza and he's a total Kayak Man. He showed us how to roll the kayak completely over and then he took us down one of those scary rapids you see in films – it was so awesome!"

That's the kind of fun time we should be having, thought Sara sadly.

That night, everyone gathered around Mr Kaminski's campfire.

If this bit goes well, things will feel better, thought Sara, hopefully.

The class ate hot dogs and cake around the campfire and cheered when Mrs Coats announced that she had marshmallows, too.

"I'm not sure about taking the bus to Rosedale next year," Femi told Sara as they ate. "Maybe there's less chance of being bullied if I walk. What do you think?"

"I'm sure it's fine," said Sara. "Don't worry about it." Hearing her friends talk about Rosedale was starting to irritate her.

"Ow!" Carter cried, raising his hand to his mouth. "I burned my tongue."

Mr Ali rolled his eyes jokily and passed Carter some water.

Sara sat back and listened to the chatter around the fire. She realised all her friends were talking about the taster day they'd had at Rosedale. She felt a lump in her throat and stayed quiet. When Mr Ali finally brought the whole group together to sing by the campfire, she sighed with relief.

As everyone around her began to join in with the singing, Sara found herself lost in her thoughts. Here she was, sitting among so many people she'd known for years, feeling totally and utterly alone.

3 Orienteering

The next couple of days went no better for Sara and her friends.

The kayaking with Gazza, which they'd all been expecting to L.O.V.E., was a total disaster. Carter bashed his elbow and Femi had been so freaked out by the rapids, he'd tried to turn his kayak around and crashed into Sara. The collision sent Sara's kayak into the rapids before Gazza had shown them what to do. She bumped and bashed her way down the course all on her own, with Gazza just behind her calling out instructions.

For Sara, it had been completely terrifying. *And we're supposed to be having a great time!* she kept thinking.

The next day didn't go any better. Carter and Lexi's idea of a great time was to go racing off on their mountain bikes.

They missed nearly all of the nature-spotting tasks they had to complete. Even then, Sara might have had an okay time, except Femi just wouldn't stop going on about Rosedale. She understood he was worried but why did he keep talking about it to her? Didn't he know how upset she was about going to another school on her own? The worst thing was that none of her friends listened to her when she tried to make things better. They just kept bickering and winding each other up.

By the fourth night of the trip, Sara was feeling miserable. It didn't look like she was going to have any fun with her friends on this trip. It was actually a relief to stop trying and go to bed.

The nightly chatter and giggles that followed 'lights out' eventually faded away, leaving only the soft summer wind that gently rattled the windows in the dorm. Sara felt cold and miserable. To warm herself up, she snuggled up and imagined she was one of the glow-worms she'd seen on the night walk that evening.

Maybe I'm just the girl with the funny glasses who everyone thinks is okay until they find someone better to hang out with, she thought. She pulled the sleeping bag up over her head and blinked away tears. *Maybe it would be the same even if I was going to Rosedale. In fact, it would probably be worse because my friends wouldn't actually be my friends any more.*

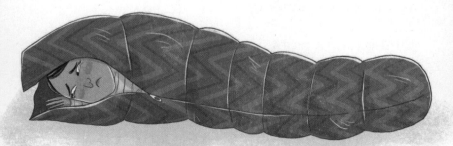

She must have fallen asleep eventually because the next thing she knew, she was being shaken awake.

"Sara, wake up," said Mrs Coats gently. "It's the last day and adventure is calling! Come on, there are croissants and hot chocolate in the dining room. There's a meeting for team leaders at 7:30, so you need to get a move on."

Sara was one of the last children up and so she was already feeling left out when she finally sat down with her team. Luckily, Lexi had saved her a croissant before the others started going back for seconds.

"Thanks," said Sara quietly.

"Today might be all right," said Femi hopefully. Lexi shrugged.

Sara bit into her croissant. It was stale.

She hurried back to the dorm, determined not to be late for her meeting.

Sara got ready and organised her bag with water and snacks. The last thing she put in was the first aid kit her mum had given her.

Mrs Coats and Mrs Wilde were both in tracksuits, looking like they'd just got back from a run, when Sara arrived for the meeting.

"Sara, here are your instructions for the day," said Mrs Coats, handing her an envelope. "Today, Alder team are going to be orienteering."

Sara remembered what Brianna had said about Ash team and how they'd all got soaked in the river during that activity. She shuddered.

"Here's the map and compass you're going to need," said Mrs Wilde, passing them over.

"There are various obstacles on this route," Mrs Coats added, "so it's really important that you get your team to work together. Okay?"

Sara didn't feel okay at all.

"Remind your team to collect their packed lunches from the kitchen and meet here at 8:30. You can set off whenever you're ready after that. Good luck!" Mrs Coats smiled and moved on to the next group leader.

Sara was relieved when her team arrived on time.

"Ethan said Oak finished this activity so fast they were back here by afternoon snack," said Carter.

"Then we'll do it even faster," said Lexi with a determined look.

"Better start by giving me the map," said Carter.

Sara gritted her teeth. She had been going to ask Carter to do the map-reading anyway because she knew he'd been to Cubs.

37

The first part of the route involved navigating a long valley, crossing streams and two steep hills before stopping for lunch. It was really tiring.

But the morning was nothing compared to how hard the afternoon felt. To start with, the team had to cross a large marshy meadow with no obvious pathways. The team got soggy feet. Then they headed into a large, ancient woodland. Carter started to lead them towards the woods when Sara asked him for the map.

"We can't go into the woods there," she told her team as a dark cloud drifted across the sun. "I can't see any tracks marked on the map there, so we might get lost. I think we should head south and cut into the woods here, by this pond." Sara pointed to the spot on the map. "That way, we'll avoid the river until we get to the bridge by the activity centre."

"But that's a really long way round – it'll take ages," Carter grumbled as the first spots of rain began to fall.

"Come on then, Carter," said Lexi, standing up. "Show us the quickest way back. I'm tired."

"Are you sure?" asked Femi, wrinkling his brow.

"I went to Cubs, remember?" said Carter, waving his hand at Femi. "I know this stuff."

Sara hesitated as her friends headed off. Should she trust in herself and go her own way or stick with her friends?

A roll of distant thunder made her shiver. "Friends!" she said to herself as she started to run after them.

4 Into the Woods

Once they were among the trees, finding their way was okay to begin with. A few needles of dim light were still shining through the treetops. But that didn't last.

Ten minutes into the trek, it wasn't just the billowing clouds that were blocking out the light. The thick treetops were casting dark shadows, too. Even worse, as the trees around them got taller, their roots were thicker. Some roots were even sticking up out of the ground, creating tripping hazards all over the place. With her eyes glued to her compass and map, Sara slowly started to realise that they were lost.

"We need to turn back," she told her friends, trying to raise her voice above the rain spattering on the leaves above them.

"What was that?" said Lexi. Her voice was almost lost in the sound of splattering rain.

Sara peered through the mist of rain and thought she saw a swish of movement in the undergrowth.

"Something's out there," said Femi, gripping Lexi's arm.

"I told you this place was full of wild animals," said Carter, his eyes widening. "This is exactly what I came here for."

They waited and hunted with their eyes but nothing moved. Then there was a sound. It was short. Like a grunt. Only deeper.

"Follow me," said Carter as he slowly started to move towards the sound.

Sara froze. What was it? She watched in terror as Carter and the others began to move away from her with every stride.

"Aaaagghhh!"

Sara flinched and saw her friends pelting back towards her, screaming.

"Run!" squealed Lexi as she passed Sara.

In a panic, Sara turned and ran too. Tripping and toppling, Sara somehow managed not to fall. With the sound of fast, pounding footsteps behind her, she spotted a tree with a hollow trunk. She stumbled towards it and squeezed herself inside. Squashed up with her backpack inside the tree, Sara caught a quick glimpse of something charging past.

What was that? She trembled.

Whatever it was, it had followed her friends. As soon as she dared, she peered out anxiously, hoping to see the others. Instead, she saw a hairy, pig-like creature turn and look back.

Then two tiny babies trotted up and joined it. They snuffled in the undergrowth and disappeared through the trees.

The next sound Sara heard was a human cry of pain. *Was that Carter?* Sara quickly left her hiding place and followed the sound of wailing cries. Zig-zagging this way and that, she bounded through the tangle of roots and knotted vegetation.

The sound led Sara to the spot where Carter sat on the ground with Lexi kneeling at his side.

"What happened?" Sara exclaimed as she bounded through the ferns to join them. Femi appeared from behind a tree and hurried across.

"I tripped on a stupid tree root," Carter groaned, holding his ankle.

Sara could see that Carter's forehead was grazed, too.

"We need to stay calm," said Sara, but it was taking all her effort not to panic. "I think we just got charged at by a wild boar."

"OMG," Femi panted. "How do you know?"

"Because I saw pictures of them on the website," said Sara. "The animal back there looked just like one. It had babies. Aren't they more dangerous when they've got babies?"

"A wild boar? Are you sure?" Carter groaned. "It charged right at me!"

"Maybe it was scared, Carter," said Sara. "I don't think it really wanted to hurt us."

"Carter's shouting must have made it jump," said Lexi.

"So, this is my fault?" Carter yelled. He looked close to tears.

"No," said Sara firmly. "It's nobody's fault. We're on the same team, remember?"

44

She put down her backpack and opened it up.

"Can I look at your head?" she asked Carter.

"You're just like your mum, Sara. I mean how you know all that first aid stuff," said Lexi, watching her friend.

Sara had always been proud of her mum's work as a nurse.

"I don't think it's a bad cut," said Sara, after she'd examined Carter's head. "There isn't a bruise." She then cleaned the cut and put a plaster on it before checking his ankle.

"Remember when you sprained your ankle last year, Lexi?" asked Sara. "This swelling looks quite a bit worse, don't you think?" Lexi nodded and pulled a face.

"How am I going to get back to the activity centre now?" asked Carter with a sniff.

Sara sat back on her heels. "We'll help you," she said gently.

"But which way would we even go?" Lexi wailed as she sat on the ground, hugging her knees. "We're completely lost!" She started to cry.

Sara squashed down the familiar panic that was rising up inside her and tried to think clearly. She needed to get somewhere high up from where she could look out across the woods. Then she might be able to see which way they needed to head to find the best route back.

"Femi, can you give me a leg-up to that branch?" asked Sara, pointing to a nearby tree.

"You're not climbing up there?" said Femi, peering up. "You're terrified of heights, aren't you?"

Sara shuddered inside at the thought of climbing the tree but what could she do? Carter needed their help.

"And what about the snakes and creepy-crawlies?" added Lexi, shuddering and wiping away tears.

"Ow!" Carter groaned again, gripping hold of his ankle.

Sara checked herself. She *was* scared and yet she felt determined. She crouched down to talk to Lexi.

"Please Lexi," she said. "I can't do this without you. Don't most snakes live down on the ground anyway? And I don't think there are dangerous creepy-crawlies here, are there?"

Lexi was quickly up on her feet, brushing herself down and squealing. "I was so scared about that wild pig thing – I forgot about the bugs! Ugh!"

Sara turned to Femi. "Can you help us see which way to climb?" she asked him. "Tell us which way through the trees we need to go."

Then to Carter, she said, "Don't worry. We'll get you back."

Femi gave Sara a leg-up to the branch so she could pull herself up. The sound of her climbing made several birds launch out of the tree.

"Lexi, you ready?" Sara asked, reaching down with her hand.

Lexi nodded and began to climb.

With Lexi pulling herself up to the first branch, Sara stood up shakily to reach for the next. Her heart was pounding. Sweat and rain ran down her face, stinging her eyes and blurring her vision.

"Sara? Are you all right?" asked Lexi in a shaky voice.

"I'm okay," she lied. "Just a bit dizzy."

The trick, Sara told herself, was not to look down. But that was hard. She took a deep breath and pulled herself up again, looking for something to grab hold of.

"Brilliant!" cheered Lexi, as Sara swung up a leg and waited for Lexi's push.

"You're doing great," Femi shouted up. "Both of you. Keep going up that side."

Sara set her sights on the glimmer of sky above and waited for more instructions.

"If you look up to your right, I think there's a big branch you can hold on to," called Femi.

It was slow going because Lexi kept freaking out about bugs.

"Lexi, you're the best climber I know," said Sara. "All that work you've been doing at parkour club is perfect for this."

"Yeah, but all that happens in school or in the gym," said Lexi. "This tree is a bug hotel! Sorry Sara, I can't go any higher."

49

With the support of Femi and Carter down below, Sara kept climbing. She pulled her way higher up the tree, wiping off bugs and checking for snakes every step of the way.

Sara was almost able to stand up and push her head into the light when her foot slipped a little. As she reached out in panic to grab a branch, she glanced down.

"Woah!" she screamed, her vision spinning like a whirlpool.

Sara slammed her eyes shut and gripped on to the branch. Her hands felt clammy and shaky. Her heart was racing.

Stop and take a deep breath, she told herself, gritting her teeth.

A steady warbling sound nearby distracted her. The noise steadied her nerves. She took an extra deep breath. When she opened her eyes, she saw a small, green-coloured bird in the tree opposite. The bird seemed to study her for a moment before it launched itself up into the sky.

Sara was suddenly struck with just how out of place she was. She had climbed a tree! Sara, the girl who got dizzy looking out of a window! How had this happened? She thought about turning back before she climbed too high and completely freaked out.

But I have to keep going, she told herself. *For Carter.*

She wiped her clammy hands on her T-shirt and took another deep breath. With one last almighty effort, Sara heaved herself up on to the thick branch above, just as the sun emerged from behind the clouds.

At first the light was so dazzling, Sara had to close her eyes. She felt like she was standing at the top of the world. "I did it," she said to herself, shielding her eyes.

"Can you see where we are and hurry up?" called Lexi from below. "There are little spiders everywhere."

Sara's eyes slowly became accustomed to the sunlight. At first, she could see nothing but treetops and green fields. She saw a huge bird of prey swooping above the woods and she gasped at its beauty. Then, straining her eyes, she peered further out. In the distance she saw something she recognised.

"I can see Rockford Falls!" she called down, checking her compass. "I know where we are."

What Sara didn't share with her friends was how far away they were. Not only that, they were going to have to cross the river to get back. The very river they would have avoided if they'd taken her route in the first place.

It took a lot longer to climb down the tree than it had taken to climb up. Sara didn't notice she was trembling all over until she was almost at the bottom.

"Nearly there," called Femi. "Now turn around and use the branch behind you. It looks stronger."

Sara and Lexi took the last jump down together, holding hands.

"You did it!" cheered Lexi, giving Sara a hug. Then Sara's knees buckled and she collapsed on to the ground, pulling a giggling Lexi down with her.

"That was amazing!" said Femi with a grin.

"That was properly brave," said Carter, struggling to get up. "Especially if you were scared of heights." He looked at Lexi, who was frantically brushing down her top. "And bugs," he added.

But Sara wasn't in the mood for celebration. She was looking at the pain on Carter's face as he tried to stand. She brushed herself down and shakily got to her feet.

"We're not out of the woods yet," she told her friends. "Let's get moving."

5 The Long Trek Home

Once Sara and Femi were supporting Carter on their shoulders, Sara checked her compass.

"Lexi, if you can find a stick and start hacking out a path, we need to head that way," she said, pointing.

"Ow!" cried Carter as soon as he took his first hobbling steps. "I can't do this!"

Sara's heart sank. If Carter was in pain even with their support, how were they ever going to get back to the centre?

"Femi, Lexi – can you help Carter on to my back?" said Sara, as she crouched down. "I'll carry him as far as I can and then we'll swap."

Lexi and Femi helped Carter on to Sara's back.

When Sara realised just how heavy Carter was, she felt her spirits dip. Maybe this idea was just not going to work at all.

"What time is it?" asked Sara.

"It's 4:15," said Lexi, checking her watch. "Why?"

Sara hesitated. "I just wanted to know." She didn't want to tell them how far they had to go.

"Well, I hope we get back soon," Carter groaned, "I'm hungry now."

Femi and Lexi whacked their sticks against the undergrowth to make a path. Sara hobbled on behind them with Carter on her back.

The problem was that after the rain the ground was muddy. Sara's feet kept sticking and slipping. Her heart was sinking too. They were going so slowly, Sara wasn't sure if they would make it back before sunset.

"Snake!" screamed Lexi, freezing in her tracks.

"Where?" gasped Carter, peering to look.

Sara winced under the strain of Carter's weight.

"I bet it was an adder," said Carter. "I'd give anything to see one. They're poisonous."

"Carter!" said Sara. "Just stop."

"I'll go in front," Femi told Lexi. "Can you trample things down after me?"

They trudged on. After ten minutes, Sara asked Femi to take over the carrying.

"Can you stop bouncing me around so much?" Carter moaned.

"Lexi – can you have a go?" Femi called. "Carter's getting on my nerves."

"What's that?" hissed Lexi, pointing.

Sara's eyes shot around and for a moment she found herself staring into the eyes of a beautiful deer.

"Wow!" gasped Femi. "Look at the antlers on that thing!"

Carter slipped from Femi's back and landed in the mud with a thud. The deer turned and sprang away into the forest.

"This is hopeless!" sighed Lexi.

"He's too heavy!" Femi complained.

Sara was surprised by how calm she felt.

"We could make a stretcher," she said. "That way we could all carry him."

"How?" gasped Femi.

"Carter?" said Sara. "You went to Cubs, right? What do you think?"

"I dunno!" said Carter. "I didn't get the 'how to make a stretcher' badge."

58

"Just which badges *did* you get?" sighed Lexi sarcastically.

"Okay," said Sara, thinking hard. "One of us can carry his arms and someone else can lift his legs." She pointed to show what she meant.

She stood behind Carter to lift him under his arms as Femi put his hands under Carter's knees.

"Just try not to wobble me around too much," said Carter.

Now that Carter's weight was shared between them and with Lexi clearing a path, they moved through the forest much faster. With several breaks for rests, Sara used her compass to lead her friends towards the light.

"I can hear running water," Femi panted, as they made their way out of the forest.

"It's the river!" Lexi groaned.

Sara felt her friend's mood change in an instant.

"How are we going to get across that?" asked Carter, as they gently placed him on the ground.

Sara didn't need the map now. She'd known this problem was coming.

"If we can find shallow water it should be easier to cross," she said, looking at her friends.

She reached in her bag for her binoculars and looked up the river. She knew there was no bridge for miles. Hopefully there would be a safe place to cross by foot.

"Got it!" she cried when she saw a herd of cows standing in the river, drinking.

Lifting Carter with Femi again, Sara led her team up the riverbank. She hoped that the cows might leave when they saw them coming, but they didn't.

"I think I'm more scared of cows than snakes," said Lexi as they approached.

"We'll keep as far away as we can," said Sara, feeling a bit nervous herself.

"Hang on, Carter," she said as they splashed into the water. "We're nearly there."

They were halfway across when one of the cows let out a very loud MOO!

"Aaaagh!" shouted Femi, jumping out of his skin and dropping Carter's legs in the river.

"Ow!" yelled Carter, as he landed on the river bed. Then, he looked up at his friends and started to laugh. Lexi doubled over with laughter and dropped to her knees, splashing the water with her hands. Sara had to hold her stomach, she was laughing so much.

Eventually, they managed to lift a soaking wet Carter out of the river and splash out the other side, still stopping to giggle now and then.

Sara and her friends were cold, wet and hungry when they finally trudged up to the activity centre. Carter was starting to feel very heavy and wouldn't stop wriggling. But they were all beaming. Several of their classmates came sprinting across to meet them.

"What happened to Carter?" exclaimed Brianna.

"We got chased by a wolf," Carter said with a grin. Then to Sara he whispered, "Back me up. We can't tell them it was a little hairy pig – they'd laugh."

"But wolves don't live in this country!" said Ethan.

"It must've escaped from the zoo," said Carter. "How did you *not* know that?"

Sara pitched in with the others as they told their story and laughed about their adventure.

It wasn't long before Mrs Coats had checked Carter's injuries.

"Seems like you've been well cared for," she told him.

"That's because I'm in a great team," Carter told her. "You better tell the other teachers so we win this best team thing."

Mrs Coats laughed.

"Well, you've got half an hour to get your team ready for tonight's barbecue," Mrs Coats told Sara with a smile. "So, I suggest you hurry up."

Meg from the activity centre lent Carter a pair of crutches, while Mr Ali offered to help him get dry and changed. The others returned to the dorms to get ready themselves.

None of Mr Ali's Year 6 class had expected the final barbecue that evening to take place down at the lakeside. As the children gathered, Mrs Wilde and the teachers were huddled up in discussion with Meg and her staff.

"I bet we've won the prize for best team," said Carter. "I hope it's something big."

They all linked arms to wait for the result.

"Right, everyone," Mrs Wilde started, clapping her hands to get everyone's attention. "Before we get down to the serious business of eating and dancing ..."

"Dancing?" Carter called out, his face screwed up. "You're kidding. Don't tell me I've got to sit here like a lemon and watch teachers *dancing*?"

Just about everyone laughed at that.

"Yes, Carter, I'm afraid you do," said Mrs Wilde. "And if you're not careful, I might have a dance with you myself. Crutches or no crutches."

Carter's face froze for a moment and then he cracked up along with everyone else.

"But now," Mrs Wilde continued. "It's time to award the prize for the team of the week. Over to you, Mr Ali."

Sara felt Lexi grip her arm.

"If we win this, it's all thanks to you, Sara," Lexi whispered as Mr Ali stepped forwards. Sara's heart began to pound. Could her team have done it?

Mr Ali started speaking, "The teachers and activity organisers agree that you've all had a fantastic week. We've been really impressed with what you have achieved. But we do have a prize for one very impressive team. The award for the best all-round team effort goes to ..."

Mr Ali paused for dramatic effect. Sara could tell by Carter's squirm that the suspense was almost too much for him to bear.

"Oak!" Mr Ali announced, holding up his hands with a flourish.

Ethan and his team jogged up to the front to claim their reward.

"Oak?" groaned Carter through the cheers. "Ethan had five in his team. We only had four."

"Yeah," said Sara with a shrug. "But they worked together really well all the way through."

"I suppose we messed up by arguing for half of it," said Lexi, looking a bit downcast.

Sara and her friends soon cheered up when they realised the prize for Ethan's team was a bag of outward bound equipment.

"I've already got a pair of binoculars," said Carter. "And who needs a compass, anyway?"

"Haven't you already got one from Cubs?" asked Femi.

"Cubs?" asked Carter with a frown. "I only went there once."

"What?" shouted Lexi. "We thought you went to Cubs for years! We wouldn't have let you anywhere near the map otherwise!"

Lexi stared around at the others with an outraged expression and then burst into laughter. They all joined in until Sara had to wipe happy tears from her eyes. She looked around at her funny friends and smiled. The real surprise was that she didn't really care that they hadn't won at all.

Mrs Wilde held her hand up then to get everyone's attention. "There's more!" she called out. "I want to talk about someone who came on this trip with no idea of her special talent."

The children started to quieten down.

"This person has been working hard all year," Mrs Wilde went on. "She has supported her friends in everything that they have done."

"You're like that," Lexi whispered to Sara, giving her a nudge.

"On this trip, this person has faced lots of personal challenges. She has led her team in difficult times and bravely overcome one of her greatest fears. I am sure this person is going to make a great leader one day. This special award goes to ..."

"Sara!" shouted Lexi, Femi and Carter together.

"It has to be," Lexi added.

"Sara," said Mrs Wilde, with a beaming smile.

"Go on," said Lexi, pushing Sara forward. "You need to go to the front. Maybe you'll get a prize."

"Hopefully you'll win more than a pair of woolly socks," said Carter.

"I told you that you might surprise yourself this week," Mrs Wilde told Sara as she handed her an envelope.

Sara felt embarrassed standing at the front while everyone clapped. It really helped that her friends were there, grinning at her and cheering.

"So?" said Carter when Sara got back. "What did you win?"

Sara opened the little envelope that Mrs Wilde had given her. Inside was a book token.

"I thought you'd get a bike at least!" said Carter. "Still, better than a pair of socks."

That night's party was the best Sara could remember. They ate barbecue food and sang around a campfire. Some of them went for an evening swim in the lake – even Mrs Wilde!

The next morning everyone rushed around, trying to find their belongings.

"I don't want to go," cried Carter as he limped out to the coach with Femi, who was carrying his luggage.

"Me neither," said Femi, dumping the bags by the coach. "But it will be good to get back to Mum."

Sara and Lexi came to stand with their friends.

"I was looking forward to this trip all through primary school!" said Sara, as they watched the driver load up their bags. "And then I thought it would never be as good as I wanted it to be."

"But it was," said Lexi.

"I could have told you it would be brilliant," said Carter. "It's obvious. We're friends."

"Are you all right, Sara?" said Lexi. "I mean, about going to Nelson Mandela High next year?"

"I wasn't," said Sara. "But I think it's going to be all right. My mum says I can start taking the bus into town soon anyway. We can all meet there at weekends, whatever schools we all go to."

"And we'll all have phones," said Carter. "So we can keep in touch."

"Can we still take Sandy for walks?" asked Femi.

Lexi grinned and gave him the thumbs up.

"If we're quick, we can nab the back seats," said Sara. "Come on!"

Chat about the book

1 Go to Chapter 4. Why did Sara need to climb the tree after Carter's accident?

2 Look at page 43. Sara 'bounded' through the tangle of roots. What does 'bounded' mean?

3 Go to pages 16–17. What did Carter think about Sara being chosen as their team leader?

4 Read page 62. Why do you think Carter said, "We got chased by a wolf"?

5 Find the sentence, '"Me too!" cried Lexi, her eyes ablaze' on page 12. What does the word 'ablaze' tell you about how Lexi was feeling?

6 Go to the end of page 65. Why has the author ended the sentence in this way?

7 Look back at Chapter 2. How did Sara feel before, during and after she went on the zipwire? How do you know?

8 Do you agree that Ethan's team should have won the award for team effort? Who would you have chosen?